Grandma Loves You

Cover Illustrated by Richard Bernal

Published by Sequoia Children's Publishing,
an imprint of Phoenix International Publications, Inc.

8501 West Higgins Road, Suite 790
Chicago, Illinois 60631

59 Gloucester Place
London W1U 8JJ

Sequoia Children's Publishing and associated logo are trademarks and/or
registered trademarks of Phoenix International Publications, Inc.
© 2018 Phoenix International Publications, Inc.

www.sequoiakidsbooks.com

10 9 8 7 6 5 4 3 2 1

ISBN 978-1-64269-045-3

Read to Me, Grandma

Illustrated by Margie Moore

When you ask me to read to you,
With your gentle voice so sweet,
I look into your bright, wide eyes
And quickly take a seat.
For in this world, I promise,
There is nothing I'd rather do
Than sit and share this storybook
With a child as sweet as you.
Of course I'll read to you, my dear,
It fills my heart with pride
That I could be the lucky one
To read right by your side.

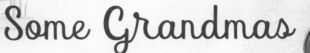

Some Grandmas

Written by Lora Kalkman
Illustrated by Jennifer Fitchwell

Some Grandmas like golf
    And some like to play cards.
Some Grandmas like taking
    Good care of their yards.

Some Grandmas like dancing
    They're light on their feet!
Some Grandmas like whipping up
    Sweet treats to eat.

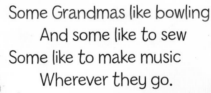

Some Grandmas like bowling
    And some like to sew
Some like to make music
    Wherever they go.

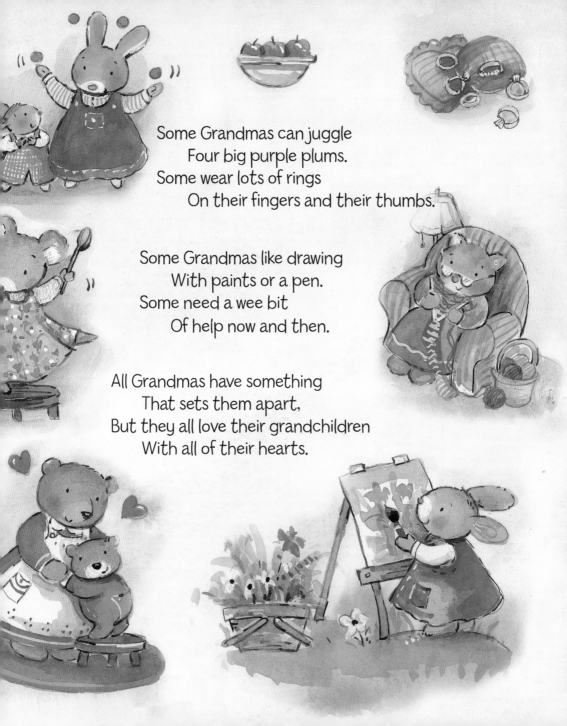

Some Grandmas can juggle
Four big purple plums.
Some wear lots of rings
On their fingers and their thumbs.

Some Grandmas like drawing
With paints or a pen.
Some need a wee bit
Of help now and then.

All Grandmas have something
That sets them apart,
But they all love their grandchildren
With all of their hearts.

A Story for Squeakie

Illustrated by Teri Weidner

It was time for Squeakie Mouse to be asleep.

"All right now, dearest deary dear, it is time for your afternoon nap," said dear old Granny Mouse.

"Oh, but my dear Granny dear, I couldn't possibly take an afternoon nap without first hearing a story!" replied cute little Squeakie Mouse.

"All right then, dearest deary dear," said Granny. "What kind of story would you like to hear?"

"A nice one, I think," said Squeakie. "One with a happy ending, I think."

So Granny went to fetch the happiest-ending storybook she could find. But when Granny reached the giant old bookcase, she wasn't sure what would be quite right for cute little Squeakie Mouse. There were big books and little books, and books with lots of different covers in lots of different colors.

Dear old Granny Mouse began to read the titles of all the different covers in all the different colors.

"*The Big Hungry Cat.* Oh no, that doesn't sound like it would have a happy ending," said Granny. She pulled out another book.

"*When You Give Me a Cookie.* No, that will just make him hungry," she said, flipping through the book. "And thirsty, it seems."

Granny Mouse pulled dozens
of books from the shelves, but nothing
seemed perfect for little Squeakie.
Finally, she spotted a book with a moon on the cover:
Sleepy Stories for Sleepy Mice.

"Perfect!" said Granny. She carried the book over to
cute little Squeakie. But by the time she got back, cute little
Squeakie Mouse was ... already asleep!

"Oh, well. Let's see about this happy ending,"
said Granny. She curled up to read the book herself.

What Do You Call Her?

Written by Gale Greenlee
Illustrated by Angela Jarecki

What do you call your grandma?
Is she Meemaw or Mamoo?
Do you call her Gram or Granny?
Mim or Pitty Poo?

Jaylin calls his gram Miss Shuga
'Cuz she smells so sweet.
To Betty, she's Creek Momma
'Cuz she lives behind the creek.

Maria calls her gram Abuela,
Or sometimes just Abu.
Boris calls his gram Babuska
And Kim likes Ludie Loo.

In China, she is Nai Nai
In Swahili, she's Sho Sho.
Some folks say Nyanya
And in Creole, she's Go Go.

But it really doesn't matter
What name you know her by.
You can call her Queenie, Babs, or Tati,
Or even Miss Moon Pie!

She could be your Ya Ya,
Your Nonnie or Nanoo,
Whatever name you call her—
She's full of love for you.

Over in the Meadow

From the original by Olive A. Wadsworth
Illustrated by Cathy Johnson

Over in the meadow in the sand in the sun,
   Lived an old grandma turtle and her little turtle one.
"Dig," said the grandma; "I dig," said the one,
   And they dug all day in the sand in the sun.

Over in the meadow where the stream runs blue,
   Lived an old grandma fish and her little fishies two.
"Swim," said the grandma; "We swim," said the two,
   And they swam all day where the stream runs blue.

Over in the meadow in a hole in the tree,

   Lived an old grandma owl and her little owls three.

"Whoo," said the grandma; "We whoo," said the three,

   And they whooed all day in the hole in the tree.

Over in the meadow by the old barn door,

   Lived an old grandma rat and her little ratties four.

"Gnaw," said the grandma; "We gnaw," said the four,

   And they gnawed all day by the old barn door.

Over in the meadow in a snug beehive,

   Lived an old grandma bee and her little bees five.

"Buzz," said the grandma; "We buzz," said the five,

   And they buzzed all day in the snug beehive.

Over in the meadow in a nest built of sticks,

    Lived an old grandma crow and her little crows six.

"Caw," said the grandma; "We caw," said the six,

    And they cawed all day in the nest built of sticks.

Over in the meadow where the grass grows so even,

    Lived and old grandma frog and her little froggies seven.

"Jump," said the grandma; "We jump," said the seven,

    And they jumped all day where the grass grows so even.

Over in the meadow by the old mossy gate,

    Lived an old grandma lizard and her little lizards eight.

"Bask," said the grandma; "We bask," said the eight,

    And they basked all day by the old mossy gate.

Over in the meadow by the old scotch pine,

    Lived an old grandma duck and her little duckies nine.

"Quack," said the grandma; "We quack," said the nine,

    And they quacked all day by the old scotch pine.

Over in the meadow in a cozy, wee den,

    Lived an old grandma beaver and her little beavers ten.

"Beave," said the grandma; "We beave," said the ten,

    All they beaved all day in their cozy, wee den.

Grandma's Hot Chocolate

Written by Joanna Spathis
Illustrated by Margie Moore

Her kitchen is toasty
And she has set out two mugs
Filled with creamy, warm chocolate,
As warm as her hugs!

It is rarely too hot
And never too cold.
But what makes it best—
Or so I am told—

Is that, besides the chocolate
And the marshmallow or two,
She makes it with love
And especially for you!

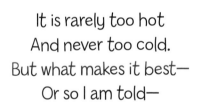